T0198818

How to give a Giraffe a Bath

Written by Celestine L. Payne
Illustrations by JJ Kirby

To order additional copies of this book, contact:
Xlibris
844-714-8691
www.Xlibris.com
Orders@Xlibris.com

ISBN: 978-1-66415601-2 (sc)
ISBN: 978-1-66415602-9 (hc)
ISBN: 978-1-664156005 (e)

Print information available on the last page

Rev. date: 02/03/2021

How to Give a Giraffe a Bath

Written by Celestine L. Payne

For my Son Paul T. Holmes, Jr.
Thanks you for the inspiration.

My heartfelt thanks to the following, Susan Pizzi my forever friend,
my artist J.J. Kirby, we were meant to be. And to all the rest
of you who continue to support my insanity!

I was asked to give my brother Raymond, a weekly evening bath

"Mom," I said. "Are you kidding me?" And then began to laugh.

How I was supposed to do this, I really didn't know?

I've only given myself a bath; I guess we could start slow.

I said "Hey Raymond, would you like to have some fun?"

He replied, "Sure thing, let me finish, I was playing tag with the sun."

"I'll bring some toys," I told him. "And even your raincoat"

"I know you need a reason to use your new sailboat."

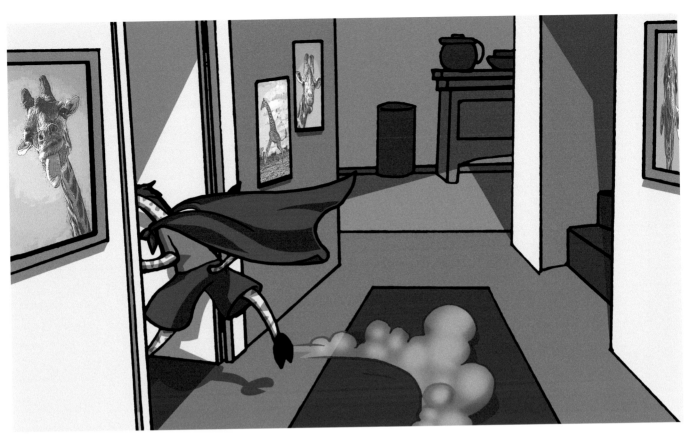

Raymond ran into his room, because he loved taking baths

Why did Mom choose me, this would be an epic task!

"Hey Raymond," I yelled, "Are you ready to get clean?"

I looked into his room, but he was nowhere to be seen.

I walked into the bathroom and there to my surprise
The most bizarre thing I've ever seen with my own two eyes.

Raymond was in the bathtub with water to his knees
He was staring at the ceiling, while laying back with ease.

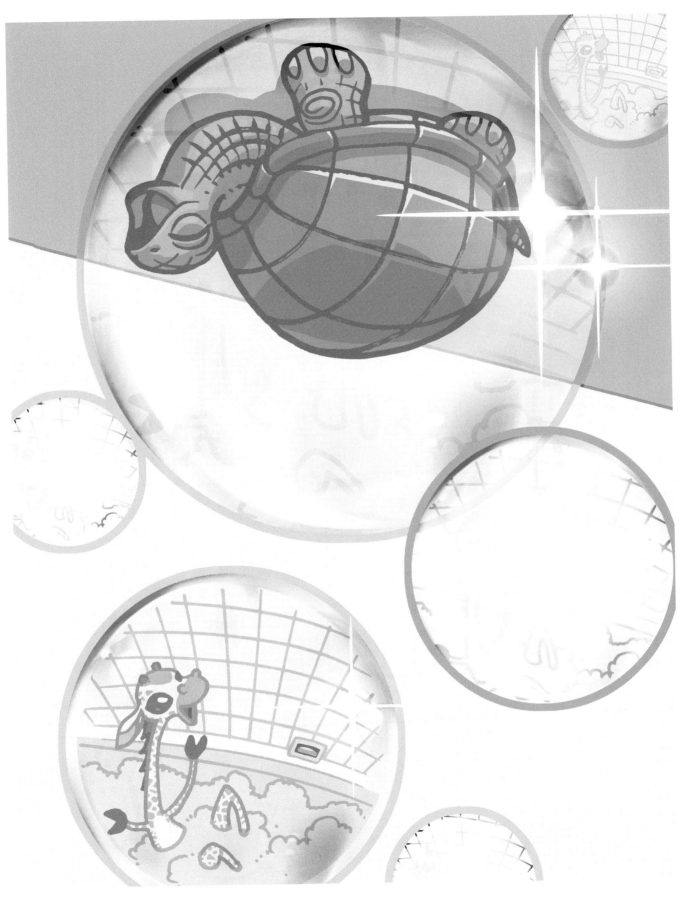

Walking on the ceiling, was Raymond's turtle Paul
Doing fancy flips, and walking on the wall.

Raymond stared at me, but I couldn't look away
I had just wanted to bathe him, but he clearly came to play.

He was fishing in the bathtub, wearing glasses on his face

I think he's done this before, my brother's a bathing ace!

Wearing one of Dad's new work boots with a green strainer on his head

Eating cold spaghetti and meatballs, there was nothing to be said.

Fifteen bars of open soap, all floating in the air
And a bunch of bubbles glowing, giving off a shiny glare.

Raymond was out of control, and he was just a calf
"I see why Dad refused to bathe you," and we both started to laugh.

"Mom, why didn't you tell me that Raymond was so cool?

"Can me washing him weekly, be a new written rule?"

"Sure," Mom said, his bathtub antics are sure to make one laugh

This could happen to you too, if you give a Giraffe a bath

How to give a Giraffe a bath

About the author:

Celestine L. Payne began writing as a pre-teen. She's taken to writing about everyday observations that she sees everyday related to her life observation. Born in the Caribbean Island of Barbados, she migrated to Boston, Massachusetts as a teen. Transitioning to a new country was hard, abandoning close friends for a new life and new friends. Lucky for her she had parents and two siblings to support her. Celestine is a single parent to a son and proud Aunt for nieces and nephews. Boston has been her home for nearly 43 years.

Printed in the United States
By Bookmasters